SCARED SILLY

Other books by
ETH CLIFFORD:

Leah's Song
(Hardcover title: *The Man Who Sang in the Dark*)

Just Tell Me When We're Dead!

Help! I'm a Prisoner in the Library

SCARED SILLY

Eth Clifford

Illustrated by George Hughes

AN
APPLE
PAPERBACK

SCHOLASTIC INC.
New York Toronto London Auckland Sydney

This book is for
Matilda W. Welter,
great editor, good friend.

ISBN 0-590-42382-7

12 11 10 9 8 7 6 5   4/9

Printed in the U.S.A.   40

First Scholastic printing, July 1989

Contents

· 1 ·
Spur-of-the-Moment
Harry

"Oh no! Not again!" Mary Rose said under her breath. She gave her father a sidelong glance. Maybe he wouldn't notice the sign that said *The Walk-Your-Way-Around-the-World Museum,* Right turn one half mile ahead. Maybe Jo-Beth, her younger sister who was in the back seat of the car, wouldn't notice it, either.

Mary Rose knew exactly what would happen if they saw the sign. Instead of driving straight ahead until they reached Grandmother Post's house, Mr. Onetree would dart off the road on the spur of the moment, to see what the museum was all about. Mr. Onetree did a lot of things on the spur of the moment. Mrs. Onetree now called him Spur-of-the-Moment Harry.

Mr. Onetree claimed he couldn't help it. Besides being a most curious-minded man, he wrote a column for a newspaper.

"About people and places," he usually explained. And he was always looking for new ideas, especially now that he was working on a book.

"Don't let your father get distracted," Mrs. Onetree had told Mary Rose before she and Jo-Beth joined their father in the car. "I'm depending on you."

"How come you never say that to me?" Jo-Beth complained. "I'm dependable."

"Not like me. After all, I'm eleven now." Mary Rose was proud of that. "And you're only seven and a half."

"Seven and eleven-twelfths," Jo-Beth corrected.

Mary Rose was annoyed. "Nobody is seven and eleven-twelfths. That's the most ridiculous thing I ever heard."

"No, it's not. If you can be seven and a half, why can't you be seven and eleven-twelfths? My birthday is only one month away. Then I'll be eight. And dependable." Jo-Beth was angry. She was tired of Mary Rose being the sensible, dependable one in the family. True, Jo-Beth was dramatic, and she did daydream a lot. Still that didn't mean she couldn't be just as down-to-earth as anybody, like her mother, or especially Mary Rose.

"Wait and see," she had told her mother. "This trip I'll be the most dependable person you ever saw in your whole life." Then she marched out to the car, jumped into the back seat, and made a face when Mary Rose slipped into the front seat next to their father.

Mr. Onetree took one look at Jo-Beth's expression and sighed. "Is it going to be one of those days, Jo-Beth?"

Jo-Beth turned her head away. How dare they all treat the Princess Sateena this way? As soon as they reached the castle, she would have them clapped into chains in a deep, dark dungeon. Let her good old dependable sister get their father out of *that* mess. She smiled. No one knew or suspected the Princess Sateena's power.

"Do you want half my chocolate bar?" Mary Rose asked. It was a peace offering. She hated having anyone angry at her for long.

"Gee, thanks." Jo-Beth broke off exactly

half the bar. Well, maybe she wouldn't have them clapped into chains, not right away, that is.

Munching the candy slowly, to make it last, Jo-Beth thought about her upcoming birthday. How she would love a surprise — a *real* surprise. Maybe a ride to the moon on the back of a unicorn, or a magic wand that could turn people into animals. Her father would be a big, brown bear, like the one that raided their camp one summer — because the bear had been curious, her father had explained. Well, Mr. Onetree was a most curious man. The image of a bear with her father's face tickled her.

What would Mary Rose be? A gentle, brown-eyed donkey, maybe, dependable and sturdy. And stubborn, too. As for herself, the animal would have to be special, very, very special, of course.

While Jo-Beth dreamed, Mary Rose spoke to her father.

"How soon will it be till we get to Grandmother Post's house, Daddy? You don't think she'll change her mind if we get there late for some reason? If we drive straight through,

without *any* stops," she emphasized, "maybe we can get up there and back today."

Mr. Onetree's eyes twinkled. "Your mother asked you to keep me on the straight and narrow path all the way to the lake, right?"

That was one of the reasons for taking a direct route, Mary Rose thought, and a very good reason. Her father was a wandering man on a trip. It didn't take much for him to leave a main highway and go exploring back roads. An even more important reason was the antique dollhouse, complete with miniature furniture, that Grandmother Post was giving Mary Rose and Jo-Beth. Grandmother had always said she would give it to them when they proved they were responsible girls. Now she had decided the dollhouse would be theirs for keeps, but they had to come and get it. She would never trust anything so valuable to the post office. That was why Mary Rose especially wanted to get to Grandmother's house as fast as possible.

Jo-Beth suddenly leaned forward. "Well, Daddy, you can't always do things on the spur of the moment, you know. You have to be sensible sometimes."

Mary Rose's mouth dropped open.

Jo-Beth swallowed a smile. How do you like that? she asked herself. You didn't know I could be just as sensible and dependable as you, did you?

Mr. Onetree held up a hand and shook his head. "Hey! If you guys are going to gang up on me, what can I do? Hold on to your hats. Here we go!"

He kept his word for the first hour and a half. They stopped only once, when Jo-Beth had an emergency and wouldn't go to a bathroom in a gas station. So they pulled up at a pancake house. Mary Rose and her father ordered pancakes while they waited. Soon Jo-

Beth came out and sang out in a loud voice that carried to every part of the restaurant, "You can go if you have to, Mary Rose. The bathroom isn't terribly clean but it's usable."

Mary Rose turned scarlet and slid way down in her seat. People were grinning at Jo-Beth as she made her way back to join her sister and father.

"I could just *die*," Mary Rose said.

Jo-Beth stared down at her pancakes thoughtfully.

"You got me plain pancakes," she protested. She reached for the ketchup bottle. "I wonder what it would taste like if I poured —"

Mr. Onetree snatched the bottle from her hand. "Now that goes against all the rules of nature. I forbid it."

"I can't wait to get back into the car," Mary Rose said. But that didn't help at all, for it was after they left the pancake house that they ran into trouble. And the trouble was, of course, the sign.

Mary Rose spotted it first. That was when she scrunched down in her seat and mumbled to herself, Oh no. Not again, and hoped Mr.

Onetree and Jo-Beth wouldn't see it. She remembered other trips when all sorts of unexpected things happened. She prayed that this time it would be just a normal, everyday car trip.

But Jo-Beth shouted in her father's ear, "Daddy. Did you see that sign? What's a Walk-Your-Way-Around-the-World Museum?"

Mary Rose recognized that gleam of curiosity in her father's eyes.

"I don't know, Jo-Beth," he replied. "I've been to art museums and science museums, undersea museums and desert museums, but this is a new one to me."

"Let's go see it," Jo-Beth begged.

Mary Rose turned and shook her head at her sister. "I promised Mommy I wouldn't let Daddy get distracted."

Jo-Beth frowned at her, and Mary Rose frowned back. It was almost like seeing herself in a mirror, for the girls looked very much alike, with their fine, straight brown hair and dark brown eyes. Except, of course, that right now Jo-Beth had a black-and-blue bruise under her left eye that made her face look somewhat lopsided. She had climbed one of the trees in the back yard, and had come down a whole lot faster than she'd gone up.

"We'll only stay a minute," Jo-Beth argued. "Just to see what kind of a museum it is, that's all. Besides," she added practically, "Daddy needs to rest a while after all this driving. He should get out and stretch his legs. That's very important for a driver."

"Why, Jo-Beth." Mr. Onetree sounded delighted. "How very sensible of you."

Jo-Beth glowed, then sent a meaningful glance to her sister. See? her look said. But Mary Rose had her head turned away.

Mr. Onetree whistled a happy tune. Both girls knew at once what was happening. Mr. Onetree was about to chase one of his will-o'-the-wisps.

"You promise we'll only stay for a little while?" Mary Rose asked.

"Of course," Jo-Beth answered for her father. "Don't be so silly, Mary Rose. What would keep us at a museum, anyway?"

Mary Rose didn't reply. But she had a sinking feeling that the innocent-appearing sign was luring them to disaster.

·2·
"Doomed,"
She Said

"What a strange road," Jo-Beth said.

"It's as crooked as a corkscrew," her father agreed.

"And so dark." Mary Rose felt a bit uncomfortable, for the car had entered a heavily wooded area. Overhead the branches of the trees on each side of the road were intertwined.

Jo-Beth hung out of the car window to stare upward. "Daddy! The sky is gone!"

"Never mind the sky." Mary Rose was watching the road, which had suddenly narrowed. Straight ahead a rickety-looking wooden bridge spanned a rushing creek. And now there was another sign: ONE-CAR BRIDGE. In smaller letters it advised: SINGLE

LANE: SOUND HORN WHILE TRAVELING THIS ROAD.

"Let's turn around and go back, Daddy," Mary Rose pleaded. "Before it's too late."

"It's already too late." Mr. Onetree drove the car slowly onto the bridge. "We can't make a turn here, Mary Rose. There isn't enough room. We'll just have to keep going until the road widens again."

"If it ever does." Jo-Beth could see it all now. The road would wind on without end. No one would ever know what became of them. They would become phantoms of the road, condemned to travel without stop.

A delicious shiver ran up and down her spine. Tears formed in her eyes. How sad! How terribly, terribly sad! *Doomed,* she thought with satisfaction.

"Doomed," she said aloud in a hollow voice.

Mary Rose pressed her lips together hard. "She's doing it again, Daddy."

"It's not against the law," Mr. Onetree replied. "A little play-acting never hurt anyone."

Just then they heard an ominous sound. Beneath them, the wooden bridge creaked and swayed. The water fled past, as if in a hurry to escape from the woods. Mary Rose closed her eyes and gripped her safety belt. She wondered if the creek was very deep. Would their bodies be lost in the swirling waters below? She reproached herself silently. She was beginning to think like Jo-Beth.

Mr. Onetree heaved a sigh of relief. "There. We've crossed and everything is fine. It was probably more sound than fury."

Mary Rose didn't bother to ask her father what he meant, for she had turned to look back. She could feel herself turning to stone, she thought. What was wrong with her? She was as bad as her sister. Suddenly she clutched her father's arm.

"Daddy." Her voice was urgent. "Stop the car." When he did, she said in a shaky voice, "Look."

"The bridge," Jo-Beth gasped.

Even as she spoke, the bridge heaved up; then, with a long, tearing sound, it broke and dipped sideways into the water below. Planks of wood ground against each other and then whirled away, out of sight.

"You and your signs!" Mary Rose was furious. If they had gone straight up to the lake, they wouldn't be on a road to nowhere, on the wrong side of a rising creek. "What are we going to do now?"

"The only thing we can do," Jo-Beth answered at once. "We just have to keep going and then call for help."

There! That was sensible. Jo-Beth wondered why she hadn't tried to be sensible before. It wasn't at all hard.

Mr. Onetree nodded. "Right. And we might as well see this museum, since we've come this far."

When it came to chasing will-o'-the-wisps, Mary Rose thought, her father didn't give up easily. She settled back in her seat. She should have stayed home with her mother and the baby. Now that Harry Two was one year old, he was a lot more fun. Right now, she hoped that Harry Two wouldn't turn out to be a spur-of-the-moment boy. She didn't think one family was big enough for two spur-of-the-moment people.

Jo-Beth nudged her sister. "Look, Mary Rose. The road is getting wider again."

A clap of thunder almost drowned out her words. The sky, which had disappeared in the woods, was black with storm clouds that seemed to drop down to hug the road ahead of them.

"Great. Just what we needed. A storm." Now Mary Rose was positive she shouldn't have come on this trip.

"Come on, Mary Rose," her father urged. "Cheer up. This can't be the only road in and out of this place. And this isn't the first storm we've ever been caught in. Look at it this way. If it rains, we'll just stay in the museum until the weather clears. When it does, we'll keep on going. I'll call Grandmother Post and explain the delay. She'll understand."

"There it is," Jo-Beth shouted. "I see a building ahead. That must be it." She poked her sister. "See, Mary Rose. Now Daddy can get to a phone and call for help, and everything will be fine."

Mary Rose stared at Jo-Beth in amazement. Was this *Jo-Beth* talking? It could have been their mother, saying comforting things to make Mary Rose feel better.

As the car rolled to a stop, the Onetrees

were struck dumb. Just ahead, a house rose up out of the gloom as if it were floating above ground. Narrow windows with tiny panes in them marched in circles around tall towers. The towers sat atop square shapes, as if a giant child had played with building blocks. Pointed roofs with red shingles sprang up in different places. Here and there, twisted brick chimneys tilted upward. At the top, some four stories above them, a captain's walk, guarded by an iron railing, circled around another tower. No part of the house matched any other part.

"What in the world . . . ?" Mr. Onetree's voice trailed off. For once he was at a loss for words.

Jo-Beth, who had a sharp eye for signs, tugged her father's arm. "Daddy, look."

Just above the doorway, a red cedar board swung to and fro. On it these letters were carved:

Harper's Abode
Where Things Are Not What They Seem

16

·3·
Open, Sesame

"What kind of place is this, anyway?" Mary Rose whispered.

"Spooky," Jo-Beth announced. "I think we ought to get out of here and never come back."

But her father's eyes were glowing. The girls looked at each other, then sighed. Nothing could stop their father now. He was much too curious to leave.

"You girls wait for me," he ordered as he leaped from the car, but Jo-Beth joined him immediately.

"I'm not sitting here while you disappear inside an *abode*," she declared. She didn't know what an abode was, but she was highly suspicious.

"Me either." Mary Rose slid out of the car

quickly. Did they think she would sit here all alone, with black clouds pressing down, and thunder shaking the sky loose?

"Come on, girls," Mr. Onetree pleaded. "I only want to use their phone." He studied their stubborn faces. "Okay." He gave in. "Though I still think it would be a good idea for you to wait until I find out —"

"Daddy," Mary Rose interrupted. "You only want to use a phone, remember?"

"And no will-o'-the-wisps," Jo-Beth added firmly.

But Mr. Onetree had already run up the steps to the porch and rung the doorbell, once, twice, three times. No one came. So he ran down again, stood back, and studied the house.

"Is anybody home?" he shouted.

Still no one answered.

Jo-Beth shivered. The house had such a *waiting* look. Was it waiting for *them?* She didn't realize she had spoken her thought aloud until her father said impatiently, "Now Jo-Beth," and her sister snapped, "Don't *do* that."

"Why don't we just get back in the car and

find the museum?" Jo-Beth asked, to make up for worrying her sister.

"There has to be a phone in a museum," Mary Rose added helpfully. "And someone there can tell us how to get out of here."

"This is no time to be sensible." Mr. Onetree was annoyed. "I'm sorry," he said when he saw Mary Rose's hurt look. "It's just so frustrating to have to turn away from something this mysterious."

"Good-bye, house," Mary Rose shouted out the window as her father started the car.

"Good-bye forever," Jo-Beth said.

They had traveled a little way, just around a bend in the road, when Mr. Onetree whistled in surprise.

"That has to be the museum," Mary Rose said.

Mr. Onetree shook his head. "I can't believe two buildings like these so close together, tucked away in the middle of nowhere, hidden in these woods."

The museum was circular, with curved mirrored-glass walls that reflected the low-hanging clouds and the surrounding trees. A large crystal dome, threaded with flashes of silver, seemed to pull the building skyward. Two huge red cedar doors, with carvings in each door panel, were firmly closed.

Jo-Beth flung open the car door and flew up the four wide marble steps that led to the double doors. Mary Rose was close behind her.

"Just look at all these figures carved in the wood." Mary Rose reached out to run her fingers over the carving nearest her. "What are they supposed to be, Daddy?"

"They appear to be people from different times in history. See here? This is an ancient Roman. And that one is an ancient Chinese."

"Here's an Indian," Jo-Beth said.

"Let's go in." Mary Rose tried to turn the doorknob. When it didn't move, she banged on the door.

"Mary Rose," Jo-Beth pointed out. "The museum is closed. Can't you read? It says so, right here."

Mary Rose studied the plaque on the wall. Her sister was right. What was happening? Mary Rose wondered. Was being seven and eleven-twelfths turning Jo-Beth into a sensible girl after all?

"Good," Mary Rose said with feeling. "I'm glad it's closed. Now we can just follow this same road and get out of here."

Her father, however, wasn't about to give up. He tried the knob, too, yanking it as if one good hard shake would make the door fly open.

"That won't help," a voice called out.

Mr. Onetree and the girls wheeled around, startled, to see a tall, lanky boy, about thirteen years old, watching them, a patient look in his brown eyes.

I wish I had red curly hair like that, Jo-Beth thought enviously. It wasn't fair for a boy to have hair that flamed even in the darkness of this day. She wouldn't want his freckles, though. She'd never seen so many — a swarm of freckles that leaped from cheek to cheek across his long, thin nose.

"We're closed today, just like the sign says. You'll have to come back another time," the boy told them.

Mary Rose stared at him in astonishment. Where had he come from? He seemed to have popped up out of nowhere.

Her father must have felt the same way, for

he asked, a little sharply, "Who are you?"

"I'm Erikson Harper. My uncle Gus built this museum. Maybe you've heard of him? Harper's Happy Hoppers?"

"Gus Harper? The shoe tycoon?" Mr. Onetree asked.

"Hey! I'm wearing Harper's Happy Hoppers. See?" Jo-Beth thrust out a foot so Erik could see her sneaker.

"Do you know anything about that house around the bend? Harper's Abode?" Mr. Onetree began.

"Sure, that's where I live. My great-great-grandfather started it. And every Harper after that added on to the house. But Uncle Gus made it what it is now."

"What does that sign mean?" Jo-Beth wanted to know. "Harper's Abode. Where Nothing Is What It Seems. That sounds scary."

Erik grinned. "Kind of gets to you, doesn't it? That was my uncle Razendale's idea."

"Your uncle Gus is retired, isn't he?" Mr. Onetree was sure he had read that somewhere.

"Sure. But he's still inventing things. He

creates magic tricks and illusions for magicians. And other things. Right now he's working on a new idea."

Mary Rose broke in impatiently. She was afraid Erik would make her father even more curious about the house and his uncles.

"Daddy. You want to use the phone, remember?"

"This is my down-to-earth daughter, Mary Rose. And that's Jo-Beth, my dreamer," Mr. Onetree told Erik. "Mary Rose is right, of course. I do need a phone —"

"And you ought to call the police or somebody," Jo-Beth interrupted, "because the bridge fell down and we have to get out of here."

There. That should show her father she could be sensible, too, given half a chance.

Just then large drops of rain pelted them.

Erik ran up the steps and reached over Jo-Beth's head. He turned one of the figures in a panel, right, left, right. Mary Rose could hear a faint click with each turn. Then Erik stood back, waved his hands in a wide arc, and intoned, "Open, sesame."

Slowly, the door on the right swung open.

"Hey! How did you do that?" Jo-Beth's eyes widened with surprise.

Erik winked at her. "Magic," he whispered.

As Mr. Onetree and the girls followed Erik through the open doorway, he flicked on the lights.

"Oooooooh," the girls said, together.

"Incredible," said Mr. Onetree.

·4·
Razendale's
the Name

"Welcome to the Walk-Your-Way-Around-the-World Museum." Erik's voice was filled with pride.

"Incredible," Mr. Onetree repeated.

Along the walls, and all down the center of the huge circular room, were rows and rows of glass cases, all containing shoes.

"Are these all Harper's Happy Hoppers?" Jo-Beth wondered aloud.

"Of course not. These shoes are from different times in history and they come from all parts of the world. And —"

Mr. Onetree interrupted, "You can't mean these are all authentic original shoes."

"Of course not. That wouldn't be possible. It would cost too much, for one thing. And many ancient shoes aren't around anymore.

But we know what they looked like. So Uncle Gus had copies made. Every copy is marked 'replica.' But we do have quite a few of the real ones."

"Why did you call it a Walk-Your-Way-Around-the-World Museum when it's only a shoe museum?" Jo-Beth asked. "Whoever heard of a shoe museum, anyway?"

"That was Daisy Dorcet's idea," Erik explained. "She said nobody would go out of his way just to go to a shoe museum."

"Who's Daisy Dorcet?" Mary Rose asked.

"She runs everything around here." Erik waved his hands around. "The museum, the Abode, and all of us, too." He smiled and shook his head. "And when Daisy talks, we listen."

"She sounds awfully bossy," Jo-Beth whispered to her sister. She didn't add what she was thinking — Mary Rose could get awfully bossy, too, sometimes.

But Mary Rose wasn't interested in someone she had never met, and wasn't likely to meet. She asked, "Would it be all right if we looked at some of the shoes while Daddy uses the phone?"

Mr. Onetree promptly approved. "Great idea. Why don't you girls get a head start? I'll make my call and then join you." He turned to Erik. "If I can use your phone?"

"Sure. Follow me." Erik walked off, but before Mr. Onetree followed, he glanced around thoughtfully.

Uh-oh, Mary Rose thought. She knew that look only too well. There was no way her father would leave until he found out all about the museum and the Abode. Even her mother wouldn't be able to tear him away from this place.

Well, it would be something to talk about with her friends later. After all, not a single person she knew had ever been to a shoe museum. So she ran off to catch up with Jo-Beth, who pointed to a card in the case beside her and said, "Listen to this." She read:

> "In ancient Egypt, shoes were worn only on special occasions by men of noble birth. At other times, a slave followed the nobleman, carrying the shoes for all to see. This sandal, dating back to 2000 B.C., was made from braided papyrus leaves, and was held on the foot with linen bands."

29

"Mary Rose! *They're the real thing*. They're two thousand years old!" Jo-Beth stared down at her sneakers. "And my sneakers are falling apart and I've only had them six months."

"These shoes are closer to four thousand years old," Mary Rose corrected her sister. "And your sneakers wouldn't fall apart either if you carried them instead of wearing them. Come on. Let's look at something else."

The girls moved from case to case. They read some of the cards, but Jo-Beth soon became impatient. She flitted from one display to another.

"You're going too fast. Come back and look at these shoes," Mary Rose called.

When Jo-Beth returned, Mary Rose read the card aloud.

> *"In Europe in the 1300s, some shoes were often two-and-a-half feet long. Most of the length was in the toe. To avoid tripping, the wearer tied the toe to his knee with a chain. People could tell how important a man was by the length of the toe."*

Jo-Beth giggled. "I wonder how long the toe would be if Daddy wore shoes like this."

Mary Rose didn't answer, for she had moved on, reading rapidly, sometimes shaking her head in disbelief.

"People were so dumb," Mary Rose exclaimed. "Come here, Jo-Beth. Look at these shoes."

Jo-Beth laughed when she read the explanation on the card in the case.

"In the fifteenth and sixteenth centuries, European ladies of fashion needed to protect their feet from the muddy streets. They wore shoes with wooden soles placed on stilts, ranging in height from six inches to a foot and a half. Therefore, the women could not walk by themselves. They had to be held up so they would not topple over into the mud."

As they moved to the next case a voice behind them scolded, "What *are* you doing here?"

The girls whirled around, speechless.

"Cat got your tongue?" the voice demanded.

Jo-Beth clutched her sister's hand in a grip so tight Mary Rose winced.

"Who are you?" Mary Rose couldn't keep

her voice from shaking. "Where did you come from? We didn't hear you come in."

Jo-Beth nudged her sister. "Please. Don't talk to it."

"I am not an it. I am a rabbit. Anyone can see that."

"We never talk to six-foot rabbits," Jo-Beth declared. "Not ever."

"Of course you don't," the rabbit said. "And quite properly so. But that's only for your everyday average six-foot rabbit, naturally." He turned to Mary Rose. "And to answer your question. I came from yonder." He waved his paw in a semicircle. "And you didn't hear me come in because rabbits are not noisy walkers. But I'm not exactly invisible, am I?"

The girls had to admit that a six-foot rabbit wearing a pink jacket with long coattails, waving a purple fan vigorously while slapping a long white glove against his leg, was extremely visible. As the rabbit spoke his whiskers quivered and his pink nose twitched back and forth.

"I'm late, you know," the rabbit confided.

"I'm terribly, terribly late. The duchess will be furious. Do you have the time?" He took a compass from his coat pocket and gave it a hard shake. "My watch has stopped at a week from next Thursday. Or is it Friday?" he asked himself, with an anxious frown. "The duchess doesn't allow Fridays, you know. Can't abide them."

Jo-Beth was puzzled, for she didn't understand anything he had said. But Mary Rose laughed suddenly.

"I know who you are. You're the White Rabbit. From *Alice in Wonderland.*"

"Clever girl." The rabbit beamed. "You got it right away. But then, I'm really very, very good."

Just then, Erik and Mr. Onetree came up to them. Mr. Onetree was astonished, but Erik said at once, "Oh hi, Uncle Razendale." He explained to the others, "My uncle entertains the kids at the Children's Hospital three times a week —"

"Razendale?" Mr. Onetree interrupted. "*The* Razendale Horatio Harper?"

"The same. Late of stage and screen. Now

in a new field. For, at last, the perfect audience." Razendale's snapping black eyes sparkled. "And always to a full house. An actor's dream."

He held out a paw to Mary Rose, and then to Jo-Beth, who shook it gravely.

"Razendale's the name, Razendale's the fame, Razendale's the game. Shall I declaim for you?" When the girls nodded, he went on, "From memory, ladies, I shall recite the information on the card in the case behind you." He bowed, cleared his throat, pressed a paw against his heart, and spoke in a deep voice.

"These shoes were said to have been carved for an ancient emperor of China. They were made from the bones of a water buffalo and inlaid with blue-green turquoise and milky mother-of-pearl. It is believed the shoes were never worn but were placed in a position of honor on a silken cushion next to the emperor's throne.

"And there, my dears" — said Razendale pointing at the case with a dramatic sweep of his paw — "are the shoes."

Everyone turned to look, even Erik.

But the case was empty!

Erik paled. "Those shoes are priceless. Uncle Gus will have a fit."

Razendale's eyes narrowed. Then he whispered, in a tone that chilled them, "So! A mystery begins! Who stole the emperor's shoes?"

·5·
Cross as a Bear, and Twice as Ugly

Erik stared at Razendale. "Who's going to tell Uncle Gus?" he asked, frowning anxiously.

"Not I," came the prompt reply. Razendale explained to Mr. Onetree, "My brother, Gus, doesn't approve of me. Never has. See, Gus has always been the dependable one in the family. I've always been the daydreamer, the play-actor. Not the least bit sensible." He laughed.

Jo-Beth turned to look at her sister. But that's exactly the way Mary Rose and I are, she told herself. Did that mean they would never change, even when they were grown up?

Mary Rose didn't notice Jo-Beth, for Razendale had continued, "So he's never really trusted me."

Mary Rose's lips formed an O of surprise. *He wasn't to be trusted.* Could he have stolen the emperor's shoes? Just to tease his brother?

Razendale clapped Erik on the shoulder. "Not to worry, my boy. We'll leave everything to our Daisy Dorcet. We call her Daze for short, because Daisy is a long name for a short lady." He winked at the girls. "Daze will be cross as a bear and twice as ugly, but she'll handle it. Daze handles everything around here."

Erik was still worried. "But what can she do?"

Razendale patted Erik's shoulder. "What can't she do? Let's go back to the Abode and find her."

"What about us?" Mr. Onetree asked.

Erik was puzzled. "What about you?" he repeated. "You've made your phone call. I've told the sheriff about the bridge. And I did explain that there is another road out of here. I even gave you directions, remember?"

"But it's still storming outside," Mr. Onetree objected. "You can't expect us to leave now. Besides, I do want to interview your uncle Gus for my paper. And, naturally, the girls and I are anxious to take a tour of the Abode."

"Then off we go," said Razendale, and he led the way to a door at the back of the museum. It opened into a long corridor, at the end of which was an elevator.

Mary Rose thought, Here I am, following a white rabbit who talks, just like Alice in Wonderland. I wonder if I'll turn into a Jo-Beth.

"Where are we going?" Jo-Beth asked. "Why are we walking in a tunnel?"

"It's not a tunnel," Erik said. "Well, maybe you could call it that. It's just a long hall that leads to the Abode. Uncle Gus had it built so we don't have to walk outside from the Abode to the museum."

When they reached the elevator, Erik pressed the up button.

"Why are we going up?" Jo-Beth asked. Now she could understand why her father had to ask lots of questions when he interviewed people. How else did you find out what you wanted to know?

"This is the first floor," Erik explained. "Daisy Dorcet has her office on the second floor."

Just then the elevator door opened. Razen-dale waved them in. "Step into my carrot patch, and we shall go forth to find our Daisy." He twitched his whiskers. Suddenly, he burst into song.

"Daisy Dorcet, Daisy Dorcet
Sews rhinestone buttons on her corset."

The girls giggled, but Erik was upset. "I don't know how you can sing at a time like this. Don't you even care that the emperor's shoes have been stolen?"

"My dear boy, don't you see? I'm laughing on the outside but crying on the inside."

Maybe he was, Jo-Beth thought. Just the same, it certainly was hard to tell if a six-foot rabbit's heart was breaking.

At that moment, the elevator stopped on the second floor. The door slid open to reveal a small woman, her arms folded across her chest, one foot tapping impatiently. When she saw the Onetrees, she was taken aback.

"Were we expecting company?" she asked Razendale. "Why wasn't I informed?"

Before Mr. Onetree could explain why they

were there, Razendale said, "Some advice, my friend.

> "Speak softly to our little Daze
> And mind your cues and peases,
> For though she has her winning ways,
> She's ferocious if one teases."

But she's not ferocious at all, Mary Rose thought. She liked Daisy Dorcet at once. She liked the short silver-gray hair that curled around her head, the smiling blue eyes, the butterball shape. Daisy Dorcet reminded her of old Ms. Forman down the street, who baked cupcakes every morning, and bought everything from anybody who knocked at her door, whether she needed it or not. Daisy Dorcet even wore an apron, just as Ms. Forman did, except Daisy Dorcet's was a carpenter's apron tied around her generous waist. All sorts of objects poked out of the roomy pockets — tall notebooks, clip-on pens, a hammer and screwdriver, a long-handled shoe horn, and some other items Mary Rose couldn't identify.

"She's nice," Mary Rose whispered to Jo-Beth.

Her sister agreed. "You're not cross as a bear and twice as ugly." The words popped out of Jo-Beth's mouth before she realized it. When her father frowned at her, her face turned scarlet with embarrassment.

Daisy Dorcet's eyes crinkled with laugh lines. "Sure I am," she said. "You just haven't seen me in action yet."

Erik could wait no longer. "The shoes," he cried. "The emperor's shoes. They're gone."

"Gone? What do you mean, gone? That's absurd," she said.

"No it isn't," Erik said, his voice rising. "You never seem to want to go into the museum anymore. How would you know if anything is wrong there?"

"I suggest you look again," she replied.

"He's right," Jo-Beth told Daisy Dorcet. "The emperor's shoes really are gone."

When Mary Rose nodded, Daisy Dorcet swung around to face Razendale. "Do I see your fine hand in this?" She explained to Mr. Onetree, "Our Razendale is quite the practical joker at times. And he does tease his older brother Gus endlessly. He has since they were small boys."

"Oh, Daze," Razendale began to protest, but she cut him off.

"Never mind." Her voice was quite sharp. "I'll settle with you later."

Why, she's not like Ms. Forman after all, Mary Rose told herself. Ms. Forman cooed like a dove. Just now, Daisy had been a snapping turtle.

Daisy Dorcet asked, "Have you had lunch?"

"Pancakes, a while ago," Mr. Onetree said.

"Then you must all be quite hungry." She crossed the hall, punched a button on a TV-speaker phone, and waited until a picture appeared.

"Mrs. Pepper, we will have three guests for lunch. One adult and two children."

Mrs. Pepper had the face and the voice of a hound dog baying at the moon.

"Children?" she howled. "What kind of children? I don't feed children. Fussy creatures. Don't like this. Won't eat that. Speak when they're not spoken to. Spill things —"

"Three guests." Daisy Dorcet had steel in her voice and fire in her eyes.

"Yes, ma'am," Mrs. Pepper said meekly and disappeared from view.

Razendale grinned at the girls. "Told you, didn't I?" he whispered.

Daisy Dorcet whipped a calendar out of one of her apron pockets, unclipped a pen, and said, "Razendale, I've set you up for a visit to the Senior Citizens Center for late this afternoon. You can decide who you're going to be —"

"But the storm," Razendale protested.

She went on as if he hadn't said a word. "The costumes have all been cleaned. The wigs are on the stands." She made a quick note on her calendar. "And tomorrow you'll be back at the Children's Hospital. Now do get out of that rabbit suit. Lunch will be served in an hour."

Razendale twitched his whiskers, shrugged his shoulders, then went whistling jauntily down the hall.

Daisy Dorcet watched him go with a thoughtful expression on her face, and deep sadness in her eyes.

·6·
The Don't Room

Jo-Beth wished she could ask Daisy Dorcet why she looked so sad, but Mr. Onetree was talking rapidly to Daisy now.

"I must explain," he told her. "My name is Harry Onetree. I write a column —"

"Mr. Onetree. Of course," she interrupted. "I see your column from time to time. I particularly liked the one on the need to save our baby seals from being killed. And that one on acid rain. One of our lakes has been affected, so that column was close to home. And the one on how museums have stolen other countries' national treasures — well done."

Erik sighed. "Come on, Daisy. He doesn't want to hear all that. Daisy's always fighting for some good cause," he explained to Mr. Onetree.

Mr. Onetree didn't seem to pay attention. He said to Daisy, "I thought I might interview Gus Harper. And perhaps write something about the museum. And the Abode," he added.

"I don't see why not. I'll get him on the intercom."

"Can you talk to anybody anywhere in the house?" Jo-Beth asked. Wouldn't it be great if they had one in their house, so their mother wouldn't have to stand at the bottom of the steps and yell up at them?

Daisy punched the speaker button, but nothing happened. "Not again," she muttered. "This thing has been on and off all day long." She turned to Erik. "Your uncle Gus said he'd be up on the fourth floor. See if you can track him down."

As Erik pressed the elevator button, she added quickly, "Don't breathe a word about the emperor's shoes. I want this kept secret until I have time to think about it."

She glanced at the girls.

"We won't tell, either," Mary Rose promised.

"Not ever," Jo-Beth swore.

Daisy smiled at them. "Erik, just tell your uncle Gus that Mr. Onetree wants to interview him for his column."

When Erik left, Daisy explained, "There are a number of things I must attend to. Meanwhile, please feel free to peek into some of the rooms on this floor."

She moved briskly down the hall, opened a door, and vanished from sight. As soon as she was gone, Jo-Beth said eagerly, "Let's go exploring before she comes back and changes her mind." She ran down the hall, then came charging back, her eyes shining. "Guess what, Daddy? There's a door down the hall that has a sign on it that says The Don't Room."

"What's a Don't Room?" Mary Rose asked.

"Let's go find out." Mr. Onetree led the way.

Jo-Beth was right. There was a sign on the door. And it did say The Don't Room.

Signs. Mary Rose sighed. Signs seemed to bring nothing but trouble. Just the same, she followed her sister and father into the room with a feeling of excitement.

"Look." Jo-Beth was delighted. "A clown."

The clown, who towered over the Onetrees,

47

had a huge yellow nose, black hair that circled his head like spokes in a wheel, huge white rings under his sad black eyes, a baggy costume held up with purple suspenders, and enormous black shoes.

A sign on his chest warned: Don't Press My Toes! So, of course, Jo-Beth did.

The clown collapsed slowly, like a balloon with air escaping. He sank down until his head rested on his feet. And all the while small, groaning sounds issued from his lips.

"See what you did?" Mary Rose scolded. "You broke it."

Jo-Beth was alarmed. "I only pressed his toes. Maybe I can fix him." She leaned forward.

"Don't," Mary Rose cried, and tried to grab Jo-Beth's hand. But it was too late. She had already pressed his toes again.

Whoooosh! The clown sprang up full size so quickly the girls had to leap out of the way.

"Come on, Mary Rose," Jo-Beth urged. "You try something. This is fun."

So Mary Rose picked up a ball that rested in a large cup. The sign under the ball said: Don't Bounce Me!

"Bounce it! Bounce it!" Jo-Beth coaxed.

The ball fit Mary Rose's hand perfectly. She bounced it against the floor, caught it, then bounced it again. This time, however, the ball moved past her hand swiftly and flew so high even Mr. Onetree couldn't catch it. Then it zigzagged around the room, faster and faster, higher and higher, hitting the ceiling and whacking the floor. As the ball whizzed by, the Onetrees had to duck out of the way. Then, as suddenly as it began, the ball slowed. With one final bounce, it fell into the large cup.

"I love this room." Jo-Beth looked all around. "What can we don't now?"

"How about those acrobats?" Mr. Onetree suggested. Directly across the room, a group of small figures, dressed in orange tights and yellow satin shirts, stood in a pyramid shape. Four acrobats were at the bottom, three others stood on their shoulders, two stood on the three, and one lone figure crowned the top.

Mary Rose read the notice. Don't Blow on Us!

The girls grinned at each other, then blew hard. Instantly, the acrobats tumbled down.

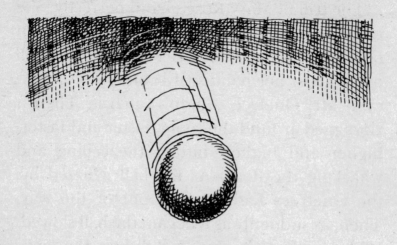

"How will we ever get them up again?" Mary Rose began when, without warning, a panel in the wall behind the acrobats slid open. A howling gust of wind drove the One-trees back against the far wall. Snowflakes swirled in, and the temperature dropped to freezing. Voices shrieked and moaned and sobbed. Ghostly forms eddied in and out.

"Help!" Jo-Beth shouted. She clutched her father on one side as Mary Rose hung on to him on the other. "Somebody! Anybody! Help!"

As unexpectedly as it had begun, the commotion ended. The wind ceased; the snow disappeared; the room warmed up; the ghostly forms vanished. The panel slid smoothly back into place, and the acrobats sprang back to their original positions.

"I think we ought to get out of here," Mary Rose said. "I think we've had enough of this peculiar room."

"Just a minute," her father said. "I want to see what this is."

He walked to the center of the room to examine a circular design in the floor. It was surrounded by a brass rail on three sides. On the design were these words: Don't Step on Me!

"Anybody want to try this one?" he asked.

"Not me," Mary Rose said.

"Not me," Jo-Beth agreed. "I don't think you should, either, Daddy."

"Nonsense. What can happen?" And Mr. Onetree laughingly stepped on the design.

At once the center design whirled round and round. Mr. Onetree grasped the rail. "Stop this thing, Mary Rose," he shouted. "I'm getting terribly dizzy."

Mary Rose searched for a switch. "Honestly, Daddy," she scolded. "Grown-ups are supposed to be sensible. You're as bad as Jo-Beth."

"He is not," Jo-Beth objected.

"Just find the off switch," Mr. Onetree roared as he spun by them.

The spinning stopped by itself, however, and Mr. Onetree leaped off, clutching his head. "My brain has been mashed into spinach," he moaned. "I've got to sit down."

"Sit on this chair." Jo-Beth pointed to a comfortable-looking armchair against the back wall.

"Daddy, don't," Mary Rose warned. "It says Don't Sit on Me!"

Mr. Onetree collapsed into the chair anyway. As soon as he was seated, two steel arms whipped out from the sides and clamped him in a tight grip. Then, as Jo-Beth and Mary Rose watched open-mouthed, the wall opened. The chair moved back, and before the stunned Mr. Onetree realized what was happening, he and the chair disappeared through the opening. The wall instantly closed.

"Daddy!" Jo-Beth cried. She turned to her sister. "Don't just stand there! Do something!" she commanded.

But Mary Rose could only stand and stare in horror at the place through which her father had vanished.

·7·
Will You Fly into My Parlor?

"Mary Rose!" Jo-Beth's bellow yanked Mary Rose out of her stunned silence. "We've got to help Daddy."

"How?" Mary Rose stammered. For once she seemed at a loss; she just couldn't seem to get her mind working again.

"I don't know. Call somebody. Yell for help. Wait! I have an idea." Jo-Beth's brain churned. "If you go through a wall on one side, you have to come through on the other side, right? Like China."

Mary Rose was bewildered. "China?" she repeated blankly.

"Honestly, Mary Rose. You know. If you dig a hole in the ground deep enough, then you come out at China. Don't you know anything? Something always has to be at the other end so," she finished triumphantly, "if we go into the room next door, Daddy will be there."

Mary Rose wasn't at all sure this would happen, but Jo-Beth sounded so reasonable, it certainly was worth trying.

The girls ran from the Don't Room. Jo-Beth flung open the door to the next room, then clutched her sister in panic.

"We can't go in here," she cried. "We'll fall off the ceiling."

Mary Rose peered in, then pulled back quickly. "There must be something wrong with our eyes. You can't go into a room with the floor up there," she pointed upward, "and the ceiling down here."

"How did they turn this room upside down?" Jo-Beth demanded. She was outraged. "It isn't natural."

"It is if you're a fly," Mary Rose said.

Jo-Beth stared at her. This was no time for her sister to be funny. Where was sensible and dependable when you needed it?

She turned to study the room again. There was no doubt about it. That must be the floor over their heads, for a sofa and two chairs were up there, plus a floor lamp that hung down, its shade facing up. In the bookcase, books were upside down. A colorful rug covered the floor — no, the ceiling, while under their feet, the floor was — no, no, they were standing on the ceiling.

"This is too confusing," Mary Rose complained. "I'm not going in there. I don't see Daddy. Let's go find Daisy Dorcet, or somebody."

"No. Wait, Mary Rose. Remember the sign Harper's Abode, Where Things Are Not What They Seem? I bet this ceiling really is the floor, and that floor up there is really the ceiling. Never mind," she went on rapidly, when Mary Rose opened her mouth to speak. "Listen. If we crawl across whatever this is under us, we can get close to that door on the other side of the room. Maybe Daddy went through there."

"Why would he do that? Okay, okay," she added hastily as Jo-Beth began to flare up in anger. "We'll try it your way. But if we fall off this ceiling, don't say I didn't warn you."

The girls dropped to their hands and knees, inching their way to the door at the opposite wall.

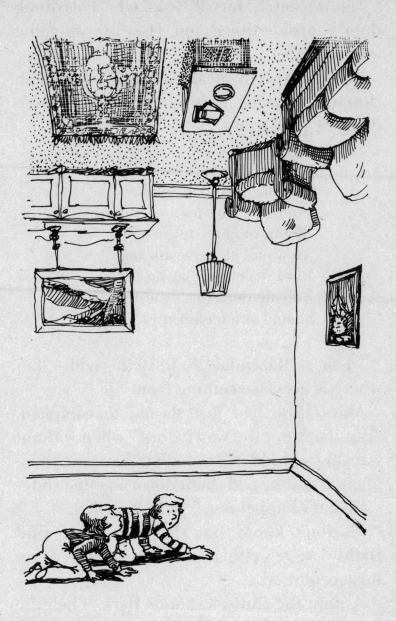

"Now what?" Mary Rose asked. "This dumb door is upside down, too. How are we going to open it?"

"I'll stand on my head and then —" Jo-Beth stopped speaking abruptly, for a voice suddenly began to sing.

> " 'Will you fly into my parlor?'
> Said the tiger to the crow.
> 'And we'll have tea and crumpets
> Before you have to go.'
> 'How nice of you to ask me,
> But I really must say no.
> I do not think that your dessert
> Should be a foolish crow.' "

"That's Razendale," Jo-Beth said, "but where is his voice coming from?"

Mary Rose had just started to complain, "But that's not the way it goes," when without warning a hidden trap door beneath them opened and tipped them down a gentle slide.

"What's happening?" Jo-Beth yelled.

"I don't know, but the minute we find Daddy, we're getting out of this place," Mary Rose promised.

At first the chute was quite dark. Then the

walls on either side lightened, and stars shone.

> "Twinkle, twinkle, little star.
> Take some jelly from a jar.
> Spread it on your little head,
> Then go bouncing off to bed."

"That *is* Razendale." Jo-Beth laughed. "He sure is silly."

"What can you expect from a six-foot rabbit, anyway?" Mary Rose couldn't help smiling, too. Spread some jelly on your head! That's what Harry Two liked to do, she thought, especially with his oatmeal.

Jo-Beth sighed. "I wish we had an uncle like him."

As the girls continued slowly down the slide, which curved gently from one side to the other, the stars disappeared. Now familiar nursery-rhyme figures appeared. A cow jumped over a moon; a little dog laughed; a dish and a spoon held hands.

Razendale's voice could be heard once more.

> "Hey diddle diddle,
> You're fat in the middle;

59

That's why you can't see
Your toes.
You roll when you walk,
And spit when you talk,
And you cannot get into
Your clothes."

"That's *not* the way it goes," Mary Rose shouted. Now she knew exactly how Alice must have felt when she wandered through Wonderland. How did she manage to stay sensible?

There was silence.

"He must have heard you," Jo-Beth said.

"Mr. Razendale. MR. RAZENDALE! Can you hear me? This is Mary Rose. We want to get out of here. And find our father. Are you listening?"

"I don't think he can, Mary Rose. I think we're hearing his voice on a tape." Jo-Beth wanted to find their father, and she did want to get off this slide, but she couldn't help a feeling of delight.

"You're right," Mary Rose admitted. "Listen. He's starting in again."

Razendale didn't sing this time. As he recited, the figure of a small, seated girl flashed onto the wall.

"Little Miss Muffet sat on a tuffet —"

"Well, finally he's got something right," Mary Rose muttered.

As if he had heard her, Razendale stopped, then repeated the line.

"Little Miss Muffet sat on a tuffet,
Knitting a sock ten feet long.
Along came a spider, who said,
   'Make it wider.
You're doing the whole thing quite wrong.' "

"You know what? I bet Razendale makes up these rhymes for the kids in the Children's Hospital," Jo-Beth said.

Mary Rose opened her mouth, but before she could say a word, the slide came to an end, and the girls tumbled onto a large floor cushion.

"Now what?" Mary Rose wondered.

Jo-Beth looked all around. Then she asked in a whisper, as if afraid someone might hear her, "Where in the world are we now?"

·8·
Take Me Out to the Ball Game

Mary Rose stood up, felt her arms and legs to see if they were whole, then pulled Jo-Beth to her feet.

"We're in the basement. We've got to be. I hate basements," Jo-Beth said.

Basements always *felt* dark, even when a light was on. Their basement at home never seemed bright enough. Mr. Onetree always promised to put in a good light fixture, but it never seemed as important to him as writing one of his columns, or chasing down some spur-of-the-moment idea.

"I guess you're right. This must be the basement. We sure came down a long way," Mary Rose agreed.

"What do we do now?" Jo-Beth asked.

"We look for a way to get back upstairs," Mary Rose said practically.

Jo-Beth sighed with relief. No wonder their mother depended on Mary Rose. She *was* dependable, especially when it mattered most, like right this very moment.

"Which way do we go?" Jo-Beth peered anxiously around. "This basement goes off in every direction."

"Straight ahead." Mary Rose sounded positive, though she didn't feel that way at all. But straight ahead was as good a way as any, she decided. If it wasn't, they could always turn around and come back.

Jo-Beth seized her sister's hand with an iron grip. "So we don't get separated," she explained.

"I wish you wouldn't put scary ideas in my head," Mary Rose complained. "Why should we get separated? Who would separate us?"

Jo-Beth drew closer to her sister. "*Things*," she whispered fearfully. "Especially in a place like this."

Mary Rose didn't know whether to snap at her sister or shudder. She didn't mind Jo-Beth's imagination most of the time, but she was already feeling uneasy, and the way Jo-Beth said *things* created all kinds of worrisome pictures in her mind.

They had hardly taken a few steps when Jo-Beth's grip tightened so hard that Mary Rose winced with pain.

"Don't do that. What's the matter with you?" Mary Rose snatched her hand away.

"Shhhh! Did you hear that?"

"You cut that out this minute, Jo-Beth." Mary Rose was angry, but just the same she listened hard. All she heard was the silence, which seemed to press in on them from all sides. Then a small sound broke the quiet.

"There! That's what I heard."

Mary Rose sagged with relief. "You scared me half to death." Her voice was testy. "That's only a clock ticking someplace."

"Why would anyone have a clock in the basement?" Jo-Beth was upset. Clocks that ticked in the dark were not one of her favorite things. And clocks that ticked in scary basements should be against the law.

"Never mind. Just keep on walking. This basement has to end somewhere."

Jo-Beth stopped walking. "I can hear it

louder now. There it is! Over there, on the left."

Mary Rose approached the clock and studied it. The face of the clock was about eight feet from the floor, set exactly in the center of what appeared to be a brick wall. Huge letters marched down each side: the word BASEBALL was on the left, STADIUM on the right. Each letter stood out boldly a few inches away from the wall.

"This is the funniest clock I ever saw," Jo-Beth said.

"I know what this is. I saw a clock something like this in a movie. Not baseball, but the same idea," Mary Rose explained. "I mean, dummies or statues or something come out of those doors." Mary Rose pointed to two doors at the right of the clock. "Then they move around and ring a bell or something. And they move along a platform and go back in through those other doors." This time Mary Rose pointed at the other side.

Jo-Beth nodded. Her sister was eleven, after all, and she knew a surprising number of facts.

The girls waited. Finally, Jo-Beth complained, "But nothing's happening."

Mary Rose shrugged. "Maybe it's broken."

"It can't be. It's still ticking." Suddenly Jo-Beth spied a switch she hadn't noticed before. "Look. A switch right near the clock. Now maybe we can have some real light around here."

"Wait!" Mary Rose warned. "It might not be . . ." Her voice trailed off as the clock was bathed in light. There was a jarring sound, as

66

if wheels had begun to turn. Then the girls noticed that the platform under the clock gave a small lurch, then moved slowly in a semicircle. The double doors on the right swung open, and four motionless monkeys came into view.

The clock chimed once. Mary Rose looked up, then announced, "It's one o'clock."

Jo-Beth didn't care. She stared, open-mouthed, at the monkeys. The first three were dressed in baseball uniforms, complete with caps, and the name The Crackerjacks across the front of each shirt. The fourth monkey wore an umpire's uniform. As the monkeys came by, Razendale could be heard singing.

> "Take me out to the ball game.
> Take me out with the crowd.
> Buy me some peanuts and crackerjack.
> I don't care if we never get back."

The monkeys sprang into action. The first one in line swiveled, turned his head from side to side, swung his arm, and pitched a ball.

"He did that so fast I never even saw the

ball." Jo-Beth was filled with admiration.

Whish! The second monkey swung his bat and missed.

The ball whacked into the catcher's mitt.

The umpire crossed his hands, then whipped them past his chest. Out!

Immediately each monkey resumed his original position and froze.

"How did they do that?" Jo-Beth wondered. "I'm going up for a look."

Mary Rose shrieked, "Don't you dare. Are you crazy?"

But Jo-Beth had already clambered up on to the platform, where she peered into the catcher's mitt. "There's no ball here. There never was a ball."

"It's called an illusion," Mary Rose explained, then realized that the platform was moving steadily, taking the monkeys and her sister toward the exit doors. "Jo-Beth! Quick! Jump!"

The monkeys had swung into action again. Jo-Beth ducked as the hitter's bat lashed out.

"Jump!" Mary Rose urged again, but her sister seemed hypnotized.

And now it was too late. The monkeys and

Jo-Beth went through the double doors and were plunged into darkness. Mary Rose could hear Jo-Beth gasp. She was afraid of the dark. She always had been. "Help! Get me out of here!" came Jo-Beth's muffled cry.

Mary Rose was stunned. She couldn't run off to find somebody and leave Jo-Beth alone inside the clock. But what could she do? Suddenly an idea occurred to her.

"Jo-Beth, listen. Try to find the doors the monkeys came out of. Just push them, okay?"

After some thrashing about, Jo-Beth found the doors, but hard as she pushed, the doors refused to budge.

"What do I do now?" Jo-Beth wailed.

"Well, the clock struck one, remember? All we have to do now is wait until it strikes two. Then you can get out."

"An *hour*?" Jo-Beth shrieked. "A whole long *hour*?"

"Let me think," Mary Rose called back. "Just don't talk and let me figure something out."

She stood back from the clock and let her eyes move back and forth, up and down. There had to be some way. . . . Her face brightened. Of course. The letters. She climbed up on the platform to take a closer look.

"Mary Rose. Mary Rose. Are you still out there?" Jo-Beth shouted tearfully.

"I'm thinking."

"Can you think out loud? Please?"

"I've got an idea. Now listen, Jo-Beth. Stay real close to the doors, and when they open, you shoot right out."

Mary Rose stood on tiptoe and grasped the letter M in STADIUM. Slowly, gingerly, she pulled herself from one letter to another until she could reach the hour hand on the clock. She managed to grasp it firmly. Closing her eyes as she swung free from the letter she stood on, she held on until her weight slowly moved the hour hand from the one to the two.

Two loud chimes bonged in her ears. Though her head rang and she was dizzy, she made her way down the letters quickly. Jo-Beth had already run out ahead of the monkeys and leaped off the moving platform. Though the music blared again, and the monkeys played ball, neither one of the girls looked back.

"Just keep moving," Mary Rose said. "Hurry."

It was at that moment that someone spoke harshly. "I know you're out there. Step forward and explain who you are and what you're doing here, or I won't be responsible for the consequences."

Consequences?

The girls exchanged fearful glances.

What kind of consequences?

What could possibly happen to them now?

·9·
Now You See It, Now You Don't

"I want Daddy," Jo-Beth whispered tearfully. "He should be here, taking care of us."

"We don't even know what's happened to him," Mary Rose whispered back.

"Well, where's Erik then? This is his house. He should know where we are. Why isn't he here? We're only little kids in a dumb Abode."

Mary Rose sighed. She wished her sister would make up her mind. One minute she bragged about being seven and eleven-twelfths and how almost grown-up and dependable she was; the next she was just a kid.

The voice impatiently interrupted Mary Rose's thoughts. "I told you to step forward."

With pounding hearts, the girls inched a little closer to the speaker.

"It's only us." Jo-Beth had to clear her throat twice before she could manage to speak.

"And who is *us*?" the voice demanded testily.

Mary Rose stepped in front of her sister protectively. She spoke quickly but clearly, explaining not only who they were and how they had come to Harper's Abode, but also the unexpected trip down the slide.

"Razendale again," the voice muttered. A man stepped out of the shadows. Jo-Beth studied him. She knew who he was the moment she saw him. There was no mistaking that red hair and those freckles, even though they were faded. Jo-Beth wondered if the man in the rabbit suit had the same hair and freckles.

Mary Rose knew who the man was, too, for she said at once, "You must be Uncle Gus. My daddy wants to interview you. Didn't Erik tell you? He was supposed to find you . . ."

"Daisy Dorcet sent Erik to the fourth floor to look for you," Jo-Beth put in helpfully.

"Well, I'm not there. I'm here." Uncle Gus gave the girls a suspicious look. "And I don't know anything about your father, either. Are you sure you haven't come to spy on me?"

"Weren't you listening?" Mary Rose asked angrily.

"Can't you see we're just kids?" Jo-Beth chimed in. She was pleased, just the same. Imagine being taken for a spy! Did he think they were grown-ups disguised as kids? The idea was so funny, she giggled.

"You can laugh if you want to," Uncle Gus told her darkly. "But you can't tell about anybody these days. Spies come out of the woodwork, take my word for it."

"But that's ridiculous. Who would want to spy on you?" Mary Rose said. "Do people spy on shoe manufacturers?"

Mary Rose tried hard not to grin, but she could feel her smile stretch from ear to ear.

Uncle Gus took her seriously. "Of course they do, especially if they suspect that you've invented something new and different. I know the newspapers call me Gus Harper, the shoe tycoon. But I'm more than that. I'm an inventor, too. Why, my Harper's Happy Hoppers were the first shoes of their kind on the market."

"Is that all you invent? Just new shoes?" Jo-Beth was clearly disappointed. It didn't sound very exciting.

"Certainly not. Are you girls good at keeping secrets?"

The same thought flashed into the minds of both girls. They hadn't said a word about the emperor's shoes being stolen, and they weren't going to; that was a secret.

"Our lips are sealed," Jo-Beth assured Uncle Gus. She loved secrets. Why, she had never told a soul that she was not Jo-Beth at all, but the Princess Sateena. Not even her very own family suspected the truth.

"Then follow me."

"Not so fast, Gus Harper." A woman moved out of the shadows, firmly holding a tall glass that appeared to be filled with muddy water.

"Not now, Mrs. Pepper," Gus Harper roared. "I have no time for —"

"Daisy Dorcet says drink. You drink. Daisy

Dorcet says you don't eat vegetables. You drink vegetables."

The girls had seen Mrs. Pepper's hound-dog face on the TV intercom, but she looked even odder in person. She was shaped like Humpty Dumpty. Her short, beefy arms and equally short, heavy legs appeared to have been put on as an afterthought.

"I thought fat people were supposed to be jolly," Jo-Beth whispered.

Mrs. Pepper had a keen ear. She wheeled around to glare at the girls. "Grown-ups talk. Children quiet. Who is not jolly? Mrs. Pepper is jolly. Listen." She gave a short, ferocious bray. "See? Mrs. Pepper laughs. Drink," she ordered, "or Mrs. Pepper not leave here."

Gus Harper seized the glass and downed the liquid in one long gulp. He shuddered. Mrs. Pepper smiled, revealing surprisingly even, white teeth. "You good boy. I tell Daisy Dorcet."

For a fat woman, she moved quickly. One moment she was there, the next she was gone.

"Okay," Gus Harper said. "Now follow me."

So they did, weaving their way along a corridor lined with boxes of all shapes and sizes.

"My inventions." Uncle Gus waved his hand at the boxes. "Some that worked and a lot that didn't. Also tricks and tomfoolery and hocus-pocus for magicians, young and old."

The girls wanted to peek inside the boxes, but Uncle Gus rushed them along. Finally they reached a large portrait hanging on a wall. A man with fiery hair and piercing black eyes glared down at them. A long black cloak swirled round his body; a raven perched on his wrist stared at them ferociously.

The girls stepped back. "He looks like he could come right at us," Jo-Beth whispered. She meant the raven, but Uncle Gus thought she was speaking about the man in the painting.

"My great-great-grandfather," he said proudly. "A fantastic magician. He was the first Magnificent Harperino."

He pressed a latch under the painting, which swung toward them. Beyond the portrait was a large, well-lighted room.

"My laboratory, built by the first Magnificent Harperino. He also built the Abode as a place for magicians to gather and create new illusions. My great-grandfather was the second Magnificent Harperino, then my grandfather, and my father after him. It was a tradition, you see. The eldest son was always the next Magnificent Harperino. Until I came along. I can create illusions, but I can't perform on stage. Now my brother, Razendale, is wonderful on stage, but only as an actor. And of course each Harperino added rooms to the Abode."

"Like the Don't Room?" Mary Rose asked.

"And the upside-down room with the slide in it?" Jo-Beth added.

Uncle Gus nodded. "And about thirty more. Well, here we are."

The girls looked around. Where were they? All they could see in this room behind the laboratory were bare walls and a large, old-fashioned, claw-foot bathtub, sitting by itself in the center of the room.

"Is that it? You invented a bathtub?" It was plain that Jo-Beth didn't think it was the greatest idea that had ever popped into someone's mind.

Uncle Gus tapped his finger against the side of his long, thin nose. "You're forgetting where you are. This is a house of illusions, remember? Now look up, and keep looking."

Obediently, the girls looked up.

"I don't see anything except the ceiling," Jo-Beth whispered.

But even as she spoke, a thin wisp of cloud appeared. As the girls watched, the cloud grew larger, fluffier, a soft puff of whiteness overhead, a summer cloud that suggested blue skies and fair weather. Then the cloud darkened. Thunder rumbled somewhere off in the distance. A streak of lightning flashed its way downward, a jagged arrow aimed at the tub. Another thunderbolt made the girls clap their hands over their ears. Suddenly it began to rain. The downpour concentrated over the tub.

The girls were well away from the tub, but Jo-Beth stuck her hand out anyway. Not a drop of water touched it.

Then, as quickly as it had all begun, the rain stopped, the cloud disappeared, and the water in the tub was gone.

"I've prepared this illusion for the Remark-

able Wizard of Watchit. On the stage, with his mumbo-jumbo patter, he will turn this illusion into something stupendous," Uncle Gus explained. "There will be curtains, and scenery, and music, and the Remarkable Wizard of Watchit commanding the cloud — all that kind of flapdoodle."

"How did you do that?" Jo-Beth asked. "How did you make the cloud and everything?"

Uncle Gus shook his head. "Explain magic and it isn't magic anymore."

"Now you see it, now you don't," Mary Rose said. "Like the scarf that turns into flowers, or the lady who disappears out of a closed box."

"Can you show us something else?" Jo-Beth was eager for more.

"As a matter of fact, I can." Uncle Gus led them back to the laboratory. He went to his worktable and picked up two pairs of shoes.

"Behold! My newest invention. The Kangaroo Hoppers."

·10·
The Kangaroo Hoppers

"That's no new invention," Jo-Beth protested. "I already have a pair. See?" She held one foot in the air.

"*Those* Hoppers." Uncle Gus waved them away. "These are my *Kangaroo* Hoppers. You won't believe the difference. Do you girls like to run?"

"I'm the fastest runner on my block," Jo-Beth said, then admitted, "except for Daddy."

"Well, try these on for size. And then run."

"Here?" Mary Rose was surprised. "In the basement?"

True, the basement was exceptionally large, but why would anyone in her right mind run in a basement?

Uncle Gus gave her a short-tempered

reply. "Don't ask so many questions. Just put them on and go around and around."

Mary Rose grumbled that her pair were much too large, so Uncle Gus stuffed some paper in the toes. Jo-Beth mentioned that hers were too small, but only to her sister. "He might decide to cut my toes off," she said in her sister's ear.

Mary Rose took the first hesitant steps, followed by her sister. In a moment, they were both crowing with pleasure.

"Hey! Look at me." Jo-Beth's face was one large smile. "I'm jumping exactly like a kangaroo. Wheeeee!"

She was, indeed, touching ground, leaping lightly forward, touching ground, leaping.

"I'm taking giant steps," Mary Rose exclaimed.

As the girls bounced around the room, Uncle Gus called after them, "This is my newest invention for runners. In ordinary sneakers or shoes, runners come down hard on the ground. They jar every muscle in their bodies. My Harper's Kangaroo Hoppers have springs in them. The springs do all the work.

No stress. No strain. And runners can go twice as far. Takes all the work out of running, but not the fun. Right?"

"Right," Mary Rose caroled as she flew past him.

"Right," said Jo-Beth as she zoomed around the room. "I'm never going to stop."

But stop she did, for she ran smack into Erik, who had just come into the room, knocking the breath out of him.

"Erik," she said. "We found your uncle Gus and we told him about the interview my daddy wants. Where've you been all this time?"

Mary Rose tried to help Erik get up. "Where's my father?" she asked anxiously. "Have you found him? Where was he?"

Erik stood up, tested to see if any bones were broken, then told his uncle in a huffy tone, "I told you the Kangaroos are dangerous. Some poor pedestrian is sure to get knocked over by a speeding runner. Daisy sent me up to the fourth floor to find you, then she called me on the intercom —"

"Is it working?" Uncle Gus shrugged. "I

turned my speaker off as soon as I came down here."

"I know." Erik sounded angry. "When I told Daisy I couldn't find you and she tried to reach you in your lab, she knew you had to be here because your speaker was turned off."

"What's all this about an interview?" Uncle Gus wanted to know. "Who's this fellow, anyway?"

"Daisy says it's okay. He's ready to talk to you whenever you say you'll see him."

Mary Rose said, "Then you know where my daddy is. Where was he? When he disappeared in the Don't Room —"

Jo-Beth interrupted excitedly. "We looked for him in the next room, and then we fell down the slide —"

"He's okay, but he sure is anxious about you two. There's a closet between the two walls. The chair stays there for a couple of minutes, then slides back to the Don't Room. Why didn't you just stay put?" Erik sounded outraged. "All I've been doing, it seems to me, is chasing after missing people. First you disappeared, then your father came charging out of the room and hunted down Daisy Dorcet. I'd just come down from the fourth floor because I couldn't find Uncle Gus. That's when Daisy sent me down here to get him, and to find you two, as well. But when I came down the slide, you'd disappeared. Again!"

"How did she know we were in the basement?" The Abode was so big and spread out, Jo-Beth couldn't understand how Daisy Dorcet knew where they were.

"She heard the nursery rhymes over the intercom. So she figured you two had gone down the slide."

Erik turned to his uncle, started to speak, then stopped.

His uncle studied Erik's face. He narrowed his eyes. "Don't tell me. Let me guess. Razendale's done something again, hasn't he? What day of the week is this, anyway?" he demanded.

"Friday," Mary Rose informed him promptly. Well, it had been Friday when they started out early this morning, but that seemed a very long time ago now.

"I knew it," Uncle Gus exclaimed. "Well, what is it this time, Erik?" Before Erik could reply Gus continued, "I knew it couldn't be a

Tuesday or Thursday." Noticing the expression of bewilderment on the girls' faces, he added, "That's the way my brother is, you see. He's only sensible on Tuesdays and Thursdays."

Jo-Beth's mouth fell open. Then she turned to stare at her sister. Mary Rose, just like their mother, was sensible every day of the week. But this was a much better idea. Even she herself could probably manage to be sensible on Tuesdays and Thursdays.

Mary Rose was puzzled. "Why only Tuesdays and Thursdays?"

"Those are the days that he teaches drama at the local high school," Erik explained. "Uncle Razendale is very serious when it comes to teaching, especially theater."

He turned back to his uncle, coughed nervously, then cleared his throat. "Uh . . . Uncle Gus . . . I think there is something you should know."

"Don't dither," Uncle Gus waved his hand impatiently. "Just tell me what he's done."

"It isn't exactly something Uncle Razendale has done. At least, we don't know that he did, for sure."

"You're not supposed to tell," Jo-Beth shouted. "It's supposed to be a secret."

"*We* never said a word." Mary Rose glared at Erik.

"*Our* lips were sealed," Jo-Beth said, with a virtuous air. She had said it before, but she liked the sound of it so much it seemed worth repeating. "And I'm only a little kid," she added. "Even if I was tortured, I wouldn't have told."

She had a clear picture in her mind of being chained to a wall in a deep, dank basement, with water dripping slowly from above, and a figure in a hooded cloak threatening her. "I will never tell. Never," she told the masked man . . .

Mary Rose broke into her sister's thoughts impatiently. "Will you please cut that out?"

"I demand that you speak up," Uncle Gus ordered Erik.

"It's the emperor's shoes." Erik hesitated, then blurted, "Someone has stolen them."

Uncle Gus's eyes widened with shock. "You can't mean that! Not the emperor's shoes!"

Erik took a deep breath. Then he stammered, "I'm sorry, Uncle Gus. There's more."

His uncle sank down in a chair next to his worktable. His face was pale. He twisted his thumbs round each other over and over again as he waited for Erik's next words.

"Before I came down here, I went back to the museum to see if maybe the emperor's shoes had been put back. At least, I hoped they would be there. But they were still gone. And then I discovered that the Egyptian sandals —"

Uncle Gus held up his hand. "No. Don't say it. I don't want to hear this."

Nevertheless, Erik plunged on. "The Egyptian sandals. They're missing, too."

·11·
The Spider Sniffer

There was a long silence. Erik had run out of words. Uncle Gus could only stare unblinkingly at his nephew.

The girls quietly removed their Kangaroo Hoppers and placed them on the table. As they put on their own shoes, Jo-Beth opened her mouth to speak, but closed it again when Mary Rose put her finger over her lips and frowned.

At last Uncle Gus sighed. "I can't believe Razendale would be so irresponsible."

Erik protested angrily. "That's not fair, Uncle Gus. We don't know that Uncle Razendale took the shoes —"

"It's a logical assumption," Uncle Gus interrupted. "You know what a practical joker he is at times."

Erik continued stubbornly, "Why would he want to take the shoes, anyway? Don't you think we ought to try to find out who else could have taken them, before we start accusing anybody?"

The girls liked the way Erik defended his uncle. Razendale was, well, different, but even though they barely knew him, they didn't like to think of him as a thief.

When Uncle Gus saw how grim Erik's expression was, he said at once, "You're right, of course. I wasn't being fair. We should be scientific about this whole matter."

Erik and the girls waited expectantly.

"I know." Uncle Gus clapped his hands triumphantly. "I have the very thing. My spider sniffer."

"You have a sniffing spider?" Jo-Beth was horrified. Spiders were icky, creepy things that walked upside down on ceilings and spun webs in corners. Jo-Beth hated anything that crawled. A spider had found its way into their tub once. Jo-Beth had screamed for her mother and then had sworn she would never take a bath again, not ever. But Mary Rose hadn't let her mother kill the spider. They were helpful creatures, she said, and she had carefully carried the spider outdoors on a piece of cardboard.

Mary Rose had done the right thing, of course, Jo-Beth admitted later, but she still couldn't understand how anyone could be so reasonable about a spider.

Uncle Gus went back to the corridor that was lined with boxes. Erik and the girls followed, curious to see what Uncle Gus planned to do.

"Can I help you look?" Erik asked, as his uncle ran his finger up and down piles of boxes.

"Don't be impatient. I know it's here."

"I don't see a box labeled Spider Sniffer," Mary Rose said. She was a good, quick reader; her glance had flown from box to box.

"Of course you don't . . . aha! Here it is." Uncle Gus pulled a box from a bottom shelf.

"But the label says No Name," Mary Rose objected.

Uncle Gus explained as he took them back to his worktable. "A man from the government came to see me last year. Very secretive. Hardly moved his lips when he talked. He asked me to invent a device for sniffing out spies. He knew of my reputation for inventing unusual items. And he also thought my background in magic would help. He told me the agency he worked for was so hush-hush it had no name. But he gave me a phone number to call."

While Uncle Gus talked, he put the box on his worktable and removed a metal device.

"When I had the spider sniffer ready, I called that number. No one had ever heard of the No Name Agency, so I just put my invention away."

Jo-Beth veered away from the table. The device set her teeth on edge. It looked like a giant spider, creepy and crawly, even though it wasn't moving.

Mary Rose moved closer. Her eyes were busy studying the device, as if she wanted to figure out how it worked even before Uncle Gus could explain it.

Uncle Gus smiled at Mary Rose. "I called it my wolf spider at first. Wolf spiders are fast runners. And they are quite remarkable hunters." He disregarded Jo-Beth's shudder.

"That's what my spider sniffer is. Or would have been, if it was ever used."

"I don't see what we can do with it," Erik objected. "We're not looking for spies."

"Spies. Thieves. Same thing. Now listen carefully, Erik. I can't take the time for any of this right now. I still have to create a rain-bow —"

"—For after the thunderstorm," Jo-Beth interrupted. "Can we watch you make it? Please?"

"So," Uncle Gus continued, as if Jo-Beth hadn't spoken, "what I want you to do is take the spider sniffer to the museum. Put it in both of the cases from which the shoes were stolen, and then activate the sniffer like this."

He pointed to three tiny buttons in the sniffer's head. He pressed the green button. "Green for go," he said. Instantly, the spider sniffer's legs unfolded, then straightened, lifting the sniffer several inches from the ta-ble's surface. It seemed to be humming.

Jo-Beth gave it an uneasy sidelong glance.

"That sound means the sniffer has been ac-tivated," Uncle Gus explained.

He pressed the blue button. A tiny blue

beam shot forward. "That's the sensor beam. It will pick up and identify the scent of the thief."

Finally, he pressed the red button. The light went out, the sniffer folded its legs, sank down on the table, and was still.

"What do I do after it has picked up the scent?" Erik asked.

"Take it to the Abode. Then just follow it wherever it leads."

Erik nodded. He picked up the spider-sniffer and turned to leave.

"Wait for us," Mary Rose said. "We want to get out of here and find our father."

Jo-Beth went after them reluctantly. She wished she were twins. Then one of her could stay behind and watch Uncle Gus create a rainbow for the Wizard of Watchit, while the other could see how a mechanical wolf spider tracked down a thief.

"Do you think the spider sniffer will really work?" Jo-Beth asked Erik.

"We'll just have to wait and see, won't we?" His answer was short and cold.

The girls could understand why. Erik didn't want the thief to be his uncle Razendale.

I hope the thief isn't Razendale, either, Jo-Beth thought. He was such an interesting rabbit, so funny and nice.

But if it wasn't Razendale, who could it be?

·12·
Up a Corkscrew Stairway

The girls had expected to spend a lot of time in the museum, but it took only a few minutes. Erik opened the display case that once held the emperor's shoes. Then, grim-faced, he placed the spider sniffer in the case, activated it, and watched intently as the sniffer sent its sensor beam round and round the case.

When it stopped humming, Erik pressed the red button. He then moved swiftly to the case that once held the Egyptian sandals. There he repeated the same procedure.

Without a word, he then held the spider sniffer in his hand and wheeled toward the back door that led to the corridor.

"Listen, Erik." Mary Rose wanted him to feel better. "Maybe it isn't your uncle Razendale at all."

"That's right," Jo-Beth chimed in. "It could be . . ." She searched in her mind for a likely suspect, then said triumphantly, "It could be Mrs. Pepper."

"Or Daisy Dorcet, or your uncle Gus, maybe. Maybe he was just pretending to be surprised," Mary Rose said. She could tell Erik didn't believe this. Well, to be honest, she admitted to herself, neither did she. She wished with all her might it was Mrs. Pepper, though.

Erik took such long strides in the corridor, the girls had to race to keep up with him. When they got off the elevator at the first floor, they were just in time to see a strange sight.

"Uncle Razendale," Erik called. But his uncle didn't hear him.

The girls were fascinated. Gone was the rabbit suit. Now Razendale wore red pants with a blue stripe and a red and white shirt, across which ran the word SuperRaz. A long, blue cape streamed from his shoulders as he leaped back and forth along the hall.

They were sure he had seen them, though he pretended not to, for he shouted, "Is it a bird? Is it a rocket? NO! It's SuperRaz!"

"He's wearing Kangaroo Hoppers." Jo-Beth was delighted. Because he was so tall and his legs were so long, he really did appear to be almost flying through the air.

"And Uncle Gus will skin him alive," Erik muttered. "Razendale must have taken them from the lab . . ." His voice trailed off.

"Without your uncle Gus's permission." Mary Rose finished the sentence for him.

She felt so sorry for Erik. This must be final proof for him that his uncle was the thief. He probably felt there was no need now to use the spider sniffer at all. Mary Rose felt badly, too. She didn't really know his uncle Razendale, of course, but he did seem to be such a funny-strange, nice man — even though he did recite the wrong words to nursery rhymes.

Mary Rose reached out and took her sister's hand. She noticed that Jo-Beth was looking at Erik with sympathy.

"I wish," Mary Rose said, and stopped.

"I know," Jo-Beth said softly.

"Uncle Razendale." Erik tried again, but

his uncle whizzed by, shouting, "NO! It's SuperRaz!"

Erik looked down at the spider sniffer.

"Are you going to turn it on?" Mary Rose asked.

"I don't think so," he answered.

"Well, I think you should."

"Jo-Beth" — Mary Rose couldn't believe her sister had said that — "are you crazy?"

"No, I'm not. You two seem to think the spider sniffer will find out that he's guilty. But it could find out that he's innocent, too, couldn't it?"

As Jo-Beth spoke, Razendale made a final leap and disappeared around a bend in the hall.

"Well, it's too late now," Mary Rose commented. "He's gone."

"It's not too late." Erik put the spider sniffer down on the floor. "It will pick up the scent, no matter what." But he couldn't bring himself to activate the machine.

"Well, if you won't, I will." Jo-Beth reached down, pressed the green button, and then the blue one. The spider sniffer unfolded its legs, straightened them, hummed, and shot out its sensor beam.

Erik and the girls automatically turned to the direction in which Razendale had vanished. But when they glanced down at the machine, it had moved the other way.

A broad grin almost split Erik's face in two. "It isn't Uncle Razendale." He shook Jo-Beth's hand vigorously, pumping it up and down until she snatched it away.

Jo-Beth grinned back at him. "Isn't it wonderful?"

"Who can it be, then?" Mary Rose wondered.

"Let's find out." Now that Erik knew Razendale was innocent, he was anxious to follow the spider sniffer. "Come on. Let's see where it went."

The machine had scurried down the hall in the opposite direction. When they caught up with it, Erik frowned.

"This thing doesn't work. There's nothing here."

"You call a door nothing?" Mary Rose was puzzled. "The door has a knob, and the knob turns. Why is it nothing?"

"You don't understand. It's a door that's an illusion, that's all."

Jo-Beth couldn't restrain her curiosity. She turned the knob and flung the door wide open. Immediately the spider sniffer zipped through. The girls and Erik followed, to find themselves in a space about as big as a small pantry. The spider sniffer waited.

"I told you. There's nothing here." Erik sounded frustrated.

"Except this door in the opposite wall," Mary Rose reminded him, "and the sniffer wants to go in."

Erik shrugged his shoulders, then opened the second door. The spider sniffer shot through and once again waited.

"Another nothing room," Mary Rose said.

"What kind of a house has doors in it that go nowhere?" Jo-Beth complained. "How many doors are there, anyway?"

"I don't remember. It was just an idea that one of the magicians worked on for a while, back when my grandfather was the Magnificent Harperino."

Mary Rose said, "I don't care how many there are. The spider sniffer wants to keep going, and I think we should follow it until we can't go any farther."

"Well, this door doesn't have a knob," Jo-Beth pointed out.

"See?" Erik said. "End of the line. I hope you're satisfied."

The spider sniffer scooted up the wall, probed the ceiling above the door, came down, then sniffed up and down the door. It beamed at a hinge near the top of the door, then crawled down to the second hinge, and stopped.

"Come on. We're wasting time. Let's go." Erik bent down to turn the spider sniffer off.

"Wait." Jo-Beth had examined the hinge. "It looks like a latch. Maybe if I turn it back and forth—" She leaped back as the door silently swung inward to reveal a narrow, steep, winding stairway. The spider sniffer crawled up to the banister and moved steadily upward.

Erik was stunned. "I never even knew this existed. I don't think my uncles do, either. I wonder where it goes."

Mary Rose's eyes shone. "Let's find out."

She shivered. "It's so creepy!" But it was plain she was ready to go exploring.

Jo-Beth held back. "I'm not going up a corkscrew stairway. I'll get dizzy and I'll fall to my certain death."

Neither Erik nor Mary Rose paid any attention.

"Wait for me," she called, as they began to disappear up the steps. She'd always hated escalators, but she'd never complain about them again. At least they went straight up and down and you could see where they were taking you. She wondered if the corkscrew stairway had been built by the little crooked man who lived in a little crooked house, with a little crooked cat and a little crooked mouse.

She almost ran into Erik, who had stopped abruptly.

"Another door," he said. He opened it cautiously. The spider sniffer went through without hesitation.

"Just look at this place," Erik exclaimed as he went through the doorway.

They had entered a large, bright room. The ceiling peaked to a cone, in which windows circled at the top. Daylight poured in, touching the two recliner chairs next to one wall. An end table between them was covered with magazines.

"Nature stuff," Jo-Beth informed the others, as she looked at some of them.

"I never even knew there was a room here," Erik said.

"Somebody sure did," Mary Rose observed as she glanced around.

A large desk was in the center of the room; papers were spread about in careless confusion. Each wall was lined with posters — long ones, wide ones, some bold in black and white, others huge splashes of brilliant colors. "Save the Whales," Mary Rose read aloud, as she examined them. "Down with Acid Rain. Smog Kills. Save Our Ozone. Don't Spray Your Breath Away. Protect the Baby Seals. Your Mind Needs Food — READ!"

While Mary Rose read, Jo-Beth's attention was attracted by the antics of the spider sniffer. It had climbed up on the desk but was now perched on a partially open drawer, flashing its blue beam.

Jo-Beth pulled the drawer open farther. Her eyes widened.

"Mary Rose. Erik. Look."

Her voice was so urgent, Mary Rose and Erik left the posters and came to the desk. Jo-Beth pointed.

"The Egyptian sandals," Jo-Beth whispered.

"And the emperor's shoes," Erik said.

"What do we do now?" Mary Rose asked.

"We'll have to find out whose room this is, and why the shoes were stolen."

They heard a loud gasp. Startled, they whipped around to see who had made that strangled sound.

There, ashen-faced, one hand clutching her throat, stood Daisy Dorcet.

·13·
A Girl Like
Mary Rose

"So now you know," Daisy Dorcet said after a long silence.

Jo-Beth and Mary Rose turned away from her to stare at Erik. His face had turned so white his freckles stood out like small bumps on his skin. His lips were firmly pressed together, as if he was trying to keep from saying something he would regret. At least it seemed that way to the girls.

When the silence stretched out, and neither Daisy Dorcet nor Erik would speak, Mary Rose said, "We thought it was Razendale."

Daisy nodded. She said to Mary Rose, though she looked straight at Erik, "Yes. I know. And I'm sorry. I had to have more time."

Time for what? Jo-Beth wondered, but Daisy didn't explain.

"So now we know who. But we still don't know why," Jo-Beth said.

The three of them waited expectantly, but Daisy Dorcet still wouldn't explain any further. She motioned for them to leave the room, then followed them after carefully locking the door.

When they emerged into the hall on the first floor, the first person they met was Mr. Onetree.

"Where have you girls been?" he demanded. "Why in the world did you go wandering off? I didn't know what to think —"

"But Daddy," Mary Rose pointed out, "we weren't the ones that disappeared. You were the one who went shooting through the wall of the Don't Room. After I *told* you," she emphasized, "not to sit in that chair. Remember?"

Before he could reply, Mrs. Pepper made a sudden appearance. Ignoring the Onetrees and Erik, she spoke directly to Daisy Dorcet.

"You say lunch for three guests. I make

lunch." Mrs. Pepper's hound-dog face was grim. She kept her hands folded over her large stomach. "Then where are they?" She thrust a thumb in the direction of the One-trees. "Children do not stay put. Not a single sensible bone in their bodies. Children —"

"You may serve, Mrs. Pepper." Daisy Dorcet's voice would have turned a volcano into an ice cone.

"Yes'm," Mrs. Pepper said meekly, and left as quickly as she had appeared.

"Is she always like that?" Mr. Onetree asked. When Daisy nodded, he said, "Then I guess she must be an unusually fine cook."

"Good enough. Did you get your interview, Mr. Onetree?"

He whipped a notebook from his pocket, then held it high as he flipped through page after page of notes. "Marvelous. What a column this will make."

"Then I think we should go into the dining room now."

She led the way across the hall, the others following in her wake.

Uncle Gus was already seated, scribbling

busily on a sheet of paper. "The rainbow," he said. "I haven't quite figured it out yet."

"For the Wizard of Watchit," Jo-Beth murmured to her father. "For after the thunderstorm."

"Remarkable," Mary Rose corrected her. "The Remarkable Wizard of Watchit."

Mr. Onetree was puzzled, but before he could question the girls, Razendale appeared in the doorway.

"So there you are, me hearties," he cried.

"What happened to SuperRaz?" Mary Rose asked.

"Can't you see? He's a pirate now." Jo-Beth recognized a pirate when she saw one. That rough black beard and the large black patch over one eye — Jo-Beth had seen the same thing on a TV cartoon.

Razendale now wore scruffy pants and a ragged shirt tied in a knot across his stomach. A wicked-looking knife with a pearl handle jutted out from his broad, black belt. Swathed around his forehead was a gaudy bandanna. A long gold earring that swung from one ear called attention to an ugly gash that stretched from his left ear to his chin.

A large parrot perched on Razendale's shoulder. The green bird opened its sharp-hooked beak and shifted from one short strong leg to the other, then settled down.

"A talking bird is a great comfort on a long voyage," Razendale said. He winked at the girls. "Still, not to everyone's taste, eh, mateys?" He didn't expect a reply, for he kept on talking.

"This is Murgatroyd, borrowed from a friend. Say hello to the girls, me bucko."

The bird's eyes glittered.

"No spitting on the dining room floor," he warned angrily.

Mrs. Pepper, who had just wheeled in a large cart holding servings of food, nodded vigorously.

"No spitting." She fixed her eyes on Jo-Beth.

"I don't spit." Jo-Beth was furious.

"Children spit." Mrs. Pepper plunked a plate down in front of Mary Rose. "Boys spit more than girls. But girls spit, too."

Daisy Dorcet spoke up sharply from the other end of the table. "That will do, Mrs. Pepper."

"Yes'm," Mrs. Pepper said meekly, and served the rest of the meal in silence.

The bird preened its feathers, then said rapidly, *"La plume de ma tante est sur la table."*

Mr. Onetree laughed. "That's the first sentence I learned to say in French, too. The pen of my aunt is on the table."

Mary Rose blurted out, "That's so silly," just as Jo-Beth giggled and said, "That's funny!"

Razendale sat down near Daisy Dorcet, studied Erik for a moment, then asked, "Is there something wrong? You seem unusually quiet, Erik."

Uncle Gus snapped to attention. "You *are* quiet, now that Razendale's mentioned it. Are you coming down with something?"

Erik pressed his lips together. Mary Rose started to speak, then clapped her hand over her mouth as she remembered their promise to Daisy Dorcet.

Daisy cleared her throat. "Please, everyone. I have something important to tell you." She stood with her shoulders back and her head high.

Razendale stirred uneasily. "Now Daze, if

this is bad news, I don't want to hear it. I never listen to bad news on Fridays."

Daisy disregarded him. She spoke directly to Uncle Gus. "I was the one who took the emperor's shoes. And the Egyptian sandals, too."

Uncle Gus was thunderstruck. "But *why?* Why would you do that?"

"It's been on my conscience for a long time. It's wrong to take a country's treasures away to another land —"

"Museums do it all the time," Mr. Onetree interrupted, "and have for many, many years. Antiquities from ancient Greece and other nations are found in museums around the world."

"That's right," Uncle Gus agreed. "How else would people get to see them?"

"It's stealing, no matter what good reasons people give for what they've done. Artifacts smuggled out, collectors paying huge sums of money to possess them —"

"Now just a minute," Uncle Gus protested. "I never —"

Mary Rose understood what Daisy Dorcet

meant. "How would *we* feel if someone stole the Liberty Bell?"

"Or the Declaration of Independence?" Mr. Onetree put in helpfully.

"Or chunks of the Statue of Liberty?" Jo-Beth said.

"We're talking about SHOES," Uncle Gus roared.

"Treasures," Daisy Dorcet insisted stubbornly.

"But what were you going to do with them?" Jo-Beth wanted to know, since no one had asked.

"Answer that, if you can." Uncle Gus banged his hand on the table.

"I've been in touch with the embassies of China and Egypt, and informed them you wish to return these treasures to their countries. They were very pleased. I expect officials from each embassy to come here a week from this Sunday to reclaim the shoes. There will be some kind of ceremony, they said. And probably reporters and other media people."

Mr. Onetree's eyes glowed. "Girls," he exclaimed. "Aren't we lucky that we happened to find this place? I'd like to be here when the exchange takes place," he said to Daisy Dorcet. "If that's all right with you. I'd be glad to make the trip again."

"Me, too," Jo-Beth said, giving Daisy a hopeful look.

Mary Rose agreed. "Me, too!"

Uncle Gus banged the table again. "Now, everybody, just hold on. Do you think I'm going to stand here and let them walk off with the prize shoes of my collection?"

"Yes."

Mary Rose thought, Daisy sounds calm. But I bet she's tied up in knots inside. That's the way Mother acted in a crisis, too. Her face never showed how upset she was, but afterward she would always admit that her stomach had turned upside down.

Daisy Dorcet continued, "I ordered replicas. Unfortunately, they haven't arrived yet. When they come, they can replace the original shoes. We have so many replicas now I can't see that it would make much difference. Most people will still be just as interested in the shoes."

Uncle Gus was silent.

"Naturally I'll pack my things and leave at once."

"NO!" Erik shouted. "No way. If she goes, I'll go with her."

Still Uncle Gus said nothing.

Razendale turned a stormy face in his brother's direction. "Are you out of your mind? What in the world would we do without our Daze? It's unthinkable. Who would run the museum? Or the Abode? Or us?"

"Besides," Mary Rose said, "you'd be some kind of special hero to the Chinese and the Egyptians, wouldn't you?"

Jo-Beth glowed. No doubt about it, Mary Rose had a good, steady head on her shoulders. That was the quality their mother saw, too.

"Where are you going?" Uncle Gus shouted as Daisy Dorcet headed for the door. "The least you can do is stand by me when all those people come barging in. You get any more bright ideas, you talk them over with me first. Agreed?"

Daisy Dorcet nodded, biting her lips to keep from crying.

"I thought you'd never forgive me."

She sat down abruptly and dabbed at her eyes with a corner of her apron.

Lunch was quickly eaten. Mrs. Pepper had cleared some of the dishes during the meal, and then left the room without returning.

A relieved and smiling Erik, his equally relieved uncles, Razendale and Gus, and a beaming Daisy Dorcet walked the Onetrees back through the corridor to the museum.

"We'll see you next week," Daisy Dorcet said, her eyes shining.

Uncle Razendale shook hands with the girls, then poked the bird. "Say a nice good-bye," he instructed.

The parrot squawked. "Remember," he said severely, "dead men don't bite."

Good-byes were said all around, and then Erik walked them to their car. The sun shone; puddles of water shimmered brightly.

The girls hung out the windows and waved good-bye to Erik. Then they watched the museum disappear from sight as they turned around the bend. Now the Abode came into view.

"What a strange house," Mary Rose said.

"Maybe we can see some other rooms when we come back," Jo-Beth said eagerly.

"Maybe." Mr. Onetree turned to his older daughter. "Mary Rose, you're so good at directions. Did Erik say a right turn or left?"

"Right, Daddy." Mary Rose sighed deeply. Who would have thought that a trip to Grandmother Post's house to pick up an antique dollhouse would become so complicated? But that was what happened when Daddy was driving. He was surely a wandering man. Still, that was what made Daddy so interesting. And though she often grew impatient with her sister, she wouldn't really want Jo-Beth to change, either.

Jo-Beth was also busy thinking as she leaned her head contentedly against the back of her seat.

When they were home again, with the dollhouse and all the miniature furniture, she would pick two days to be sensible. Well, maybe not. She should probably just start off with one day, and then work her way up to two.

How did Mary Rose manage to be sensible all the time?

Well, if you were going to have an adventure like the one they had this day, there was nothing better than having it with a responsible, dependable, *sensible* girl like Mary Rose.